I0766483

In Defense of Big Dreams

words by Mackenzie Myatt

photography by Artúr Sagát

Dedication

This book is for girls everywhere with big dreams. For everyone who wonders if their dream is too big, they've outgrown it, or given up on an old dream altogether. This book is for falling in love with your passion - again. Falling in love with what makes you tick and being honest about what doesn't. This book is for not being afraid to change direction, to question everything.

It took me a long time to realize my relationship with cycling wasn't making me happy anymore and it had to change. So I decided to change.

Publishing a book is a dream I'd given up on a long time ago, yet here I am. I thought if I didn't decide to be a writer after my writing degree, that it wasn't going to happen. I didn't know what kind of writer I wanted to be. I thought I had to be a literary writer or a journalist and when neither of those things called to me, I felt lost. But sometimes the most obvious answer is the best one.

What do I love to do? Write poetry and ride my bike.

Poetry licks the
part of me that
feels like it's
dying and
suddenly I'm
wide awake.

Nothing on Netflix

There's nothing for me on Netflix
That feels like poetry.
That feels like romance without so much cheese
You couldn't grate it to be
More palatable
If you tried.
I need something that speaks to me slowly
Not eloquently
But in defense of big dreams
And the small things that bother me
Something beautiful that inspires me
To write about why it's not always good to be youthful
But I want to be soothed too
I want to be moved to say
Something useful
I want you to hear the rhyme
And be so swept up you lose
Track of time
Poetry licks the part of me
that feels like it's dying
and suddenly I'm wide awake.

Tell me where you can find that on Netflix.

Be Strong

When I say be strong
I mean
Be permeable
Let life wash over you
And leave you only with treasure
A wave is only strong until it breaks
And then it wakes up the world
I want you to always be brave enough
To be brave again
When you need to
You don't have to be spritely
Or excited
In the early hours
But there should be something that makes hours feel
Like minutes
Something so riveting
It fills your senses with buckets of bravery
Something sweet, salty and savory

When I say be strong
I mean be audacious
Voracious
Graceful in defeat
When it's hailing
When it feels like someone
Ripped a hole in your sails
When it feels like the gale is against you
That's when you hunker down
And let stubbornness guide you
Don't give up on ideas that are so bright
They blind you
When I say be strong
I mean
Don't be afraid
To be wrong.

When I say
be strong
I mean don't
be afraid
to be wrong.

I Can't Meditate

I can't meditate
Not yet
I tried
The closest I can get
Is riding hours from my mind

I start with
Did I start the laundry
Did I wash the dishes in the sink
Are the leftovers ready
For the way that I'll be

Miles from here
Mentally
I won't be worried about everything
I'm thinking
About what I want to be
If there's anything I can change

If the answer is

Be patient
The best you can do is wait
smell the metaphorical roses
The dust in my nose
The salt in my ears
The sweat in my eyes
My legs whispering over and over
It stings

But it feels good too
The legs tick over
I have no more decisions to make
Only to enjoy the moment
Get out and get back
And when I get home
I know that most things can wait
And if they can't wait
I'll make them
Because right now I want nothing
And nothing is better than that.

Dear Dreamer,

Dear Dreamer

Don't be so hard on yourself
I know you're doing your best
You don't need tough love
You need someone who believes in you
I know how much you want this
I know how much you give up
Just to show up
And try
I know you're tired of being brave
Of doing it 'for the experience'
Of listening to everyone telling you
To be patient
Your day will come
Fuck that
A fire can only burn so long
On its own
When momentum is a ghost
You have to find another way to move forward
Don't believe everything
'Everyone' is telling you
The only thing that matters
Is what's best for you
And only you know what that is.

We Could Be Friends

If I see another woman on a group ride
I get excited because
I know what she's been through
I know she's been dropped countless times
Left alone to crawl home
Gone hungry because she couldn't reach a bar
Forgotten her chamois cream and
Regretted it every pedal stroke for the next eternity
I know she's not talking because she is putting every ounce
Of concentration
Into staying on the wheel

Watching the movement in the group
Like a school of fish
Trying to figure out which stream is this
Which elevator on the move
Which one might be stable
And which one is going down
You better jump ship before you're dangling off
The end of this thing
And you feel like a yo-yo at the end of its thread
I know the struggle so well
I could recite it with my eyes closed
Maybe if we both make it through this
We could be friends.

Potential
is a
funny
word

that
kicks me
in my
chest

Potential is a Funny Word

Sometimes potential is the shape of a cloud in the sky
It could be anything, really
It is what you want it to be
It is as blurry, as hopeful
As bright as if you squint just right you can see a shooting star
But potential is also a word that is used to judge us
To step by step
With closed eyes and clenched fists
Pull us away from our joy
Suddenly potential becomes a reason
To start sacrificing the little things
To categorize our dreams into
Let's be realistic
These are the metrics that tell us
If you'll amount to anything
And you're still too raw
We aren't fortune tellers
We can only tell you what we see

And we don't see you going anywhere yet,
Come back when you can show us some potential.
But is this thing
That kicks me in my chest
That wakes me up in the middle of the night
Excited
Smiling
Tying Olympic rings in my hair
Waking up with a purpose and a place to go
A reason to do all of the hard things
That make me feel like I'm flying
Not potential?
Potential is a natural high I ride every day,
Don't tell me I don't have any.

The Hammock Has Springs

It doesn't
But did you know
If you hang in a hammock
Long enough
It will tell you a secret
It will tell you that the sky is blue
Even if you close your eyes
That if you can find true peace
And be quiet
For a moment
The bees won't bother you.

It will tell you that suspense isn't always
A bad thing
That hanging without knowing
Which way you are facing
Actually grounds you
All that matters
Is that you're facing the sun
It will tell you
This is enough.

Suspense isn't always a bad thing.

Keep Riding

Remember what it feels like
To fly
To snap and crackle with
Energy
You are taut with potential
Relish in it
Read the room
The start line
The gap in the tape
The inside line
The wide-angle fly by
This is the reason you ride
To find the moment your limit
Turns a blind eye and says
Keep riding.

Keep Riding

What Makes You Happy Can Change.

Or at least the way you chase the
Thing that makes you happy
Should change
Because we are always changing
And that's okay
That's something to celebrate.

After: Strong is the New Pretty

You mean pretty humble?
Not likely
Pretty frizzy
Pretty freckled
Pretty sun-burned
And blustery
Pretty big head
Full of big ideas
Eyes wide with excitement
And a mouthful of what ifs
What if there's a different way
To be beautiful
What if it was beautiful
To be stubborn
Steadfast
Sticky
Picky
Silly
And willful.

Strong
Was always
Pretty.

Pretty frizzy
Pretty freckled
Pretty sunburned
And blustery.

A Cyclist Running

Is in for a surprise
It's harder than you think
But endurance comes quickly
There's nothing about this
That screams minimal gains
There's no two ways about it
I am getting faster, for longer
Like a snap of the fingers
It feels easy to only do something
three times a week
you mean I get to be fresh
every second day?
I wouldn't have dreamed it.

The only problem is things
Are fighting back
My right hamstring
And my left thigh
Are in total denial
Of this new kick called
Running for fun

So, I have to be careful
and I have to buy some new shoes

'from the top shelf'
Which is a nice pill to swallow
Compared to buying a bike
You mean the shoes don't need
cleaning
Or cleats
Or booties
Or an elaborate dial-tightening
ratchet system
That responds to low impact
With a trigger-happy eject button
No warnings or parachutes attached.

Running for fun?
Sign me up.

Running in the Rain

I drank a big, bad coffee
And blasted Tyga from the basement
I want the whole house to know
What's up
I'm not going down today
I'm not getting complacent
Not giving up
Not getting talked out of it
I like the fresh air
I don't mind if its wet
I'm not waterproof but winterproof
My motivation is waiting
Just outside the door
I know that first step is one
Of many, many more.
It's dark and grey
But each step paints a picture
There's so much colour here
If you choose to look closely
Let the tailwind carry you

The storm gusts are not here
To fail you
They will try to derail you
But if you let them
They will build you up
Slow you, catch you gasping for
air
But your heart doesn't care
You're all fired up
The weather is nothing compared
To what's burning inside
I'm not running from
I'm running to my future
Self
Each time I step out to greet
you
I say hello,
It's so nice to meet you again.

Green

Green is a trampoline
That makes my heart double-bounce
When I close my eyes
I can feel the soft texture
Of leaves on my face
Like a trickle of cold water
On a summer day
Fresh is an understatement
I could yell from the rooftops
The gentle belly-dancing of the forest
Tells me hope is a hula hoop
I can hold forever
If I want to.

Why You Ride

Let's get to the root of why you ride
It's not for exercise
Though movement is medicine
I'll preach that all day
It's for all the things you thought you could never do
Go fast or long
Be brave enough to go downhill
Pop a wheelie
Or the curb
Just gather yourself and all of your anxiety
Before you get out the door
Let's do this
Each and every one of you
That thinks it will be too hard
Too cold
Too hot
Too long

Too bumpy
I'm already hungry
I'm dehydrated
I didn't sleep well
I was tired so I had a coffee
Now my mind is on a
Merry-go-round
All of these things
But I know
I won't feel better if I don't go
So I go
And I tell myself
Go easy
You don't have to go far
Only do it if you smile in the
First five minutes
And usually
I smile as soon as I get out of
The driveway.

Bad Hair Day

I have a lot of trouble admitting
I'm having a bad hair day
I keep thinking that it's my fault
That there must be something I can do better
I must be able to fix it
With more control and more details
And more lists
But the more I try to hold on to
Any sense of productivity
The more I'm dropping literal things
Out of my hands
In the parking lot
Gloves, water bottles,
Skittles, a vest,
My sunglasses, nerves
And any hope I'm going to be able to
Salvage my training
My garmin tells me I have no heart beat
And soon after the battery gives up altogether
I have a choice here
I can give up or give in
It's that simple
I choose to give joy a chance
And just go for a bike ride
No numbers
No worries
No problem
Just me, my front wheel and
The wind in my hair.

Just me,
my front
wheel and
the wind in
my hair.

FOR WHEN THE SKY IS FALLING

A Dance Party in the Kitchen

There's not much
a dance party in the kitchen
can't fix
a dance for your eyes only
for when the sky is falling
but only you can see it
reach up into the skylight
let the music move you in a way
you haven't in awhile
don't be shy
the rhythm loves you
tapping, spinning,
sinking, winning,
this moment is a pinata of expectations
let it erupt inside you.

Motivated and Mad

Everyone talks about motivation
Like it's the key to the kingdom
How do you get it
Where do you put it
When you find it
How do you keep it from slipping away?

Being motivated is addicting
One taste and it feels like
A storm is brewing inside you
The first wave crashes
And you want it to lap forever

But have you ever been motivated
And mad?
Lord –
It's like having a hand
In a grumbling cloud
I can feel the crackling in my fingers
Crawling in my skin
There's only so long I can
Hold this power in.

BUT ONLY YOU CAN SEE IT

Rest Days are Rough

Everyone thinks rest days are relaxing
because you don't have to train
And I try
I really do
But there's so much catching up to do!

There's work and laundry
We're running low on groceries
The dishes are piling up
The bikes are dirty
The trainer is in the way,
The compost is taunting me.

I have time but,
No energy
The fatigue is ringing in my forehead
And my eyes are blinking shut.

I need help
I need
A coffee?
It's early enough
I could have a half-caf.
It might be too much
Might be asking for trouble
Decaf for delicate people
That's what I need.

It tastes okay
Especially with a date square.
Here's me pretending
I'm having a date for One at
The café called Naptime
Right next to Bedtime.

So, I tried some coffee and I felt really fancy
But it didn't elevate my mood the way I was hoping
I can feel my eyelids drooping.

Maybe I'm dehydrated. Detective electrolyte to the rescue.
Yes, my brain power is flickering but I can do this.
Let's do fancy electrolytes, come on do it properly.
I need help, remember?
Apple cider flavour
This headache wants the expensive stuff,
At least I'm consistent
Isn't that what training is all about?

So, I drink the juice and it's nice,
Don't get me wrong but it doesn't take long
To decide I don't want to work THAT much,
And we don't really need groceries right now and
Maybe I'll just rest my eyes…

It helps, but I have to tell you
I tried everything
And sometimes on a rest day
You just need to rest.

I wish someone had told me.

Woman on a Group Ride

I pretend I don't have to pee
20 minutes from the parking lot
That I definitely wouldn't have stopped to pee an hour in
Which was an hour ago
I don't dare ask if anyone else has to pee
I pretend
That I can definitely eat a granola bar at threshold
I'm not choking
I just inhaled crackers
I'm fine,
That's why I'm so quiet
I try to pedal as smoothly as possible when I'm cracked
So, no one thinks I'm a drama queen
Or worse –
A wobbly wheel
If somehow
I forget to snot in secret
I may be deemed 'unladylike'
The horror
I show up to smash myself into oblivion
With 25 Master's riders
At 7:20am on a Saturday
To brave the questioning looks,
The comments about the average speed
About how small I am, how fit I am,
All the free-flying advice,
War stories from Master's National Championships
And the one guy that always gets away
I'm not here to be anything ladylike
I am here despite you
And from now on
I will snot in spite of you.

LLYWOOD

The Work

Most people think The Work
Is the moment you want to give up
the moment it feels like the sky is falling
It's all too much
The walls are closing in on you
You're panicking
There's fear in your throat
It just hurts a lot
And that's one piece
But the work is also all of the moments
That build up to that moment
Commiting to everything
That makes the work easier
And those things are much easier
Than doing it anyway
When it's the most difficult.
Eat the right thing at the right time

So the hard things are easy to start
Wake up at the same time everyday
So you have time to play with
Drink the right amount of coffee that
Makes you want to create something
Not hate yourself
Or don't drink coffee at all
Don't subscribe to what you think
You're supposed to do
You're supposed to enjoy it
You're supposed to get excited
You're supposed to want the best
Not for the VIPs
For the MIPs
The most important person is you
And if you're satisfied
You can sleep easy
So you can do The Work
You want to do.

Molasses

I'm pedaling molasses
And my mind is on every muscle
Every itch
Finding tightness in my shoulders
In my hips
There's a twitch in my thigh
There's a bug in my eye

I love riding my bike
I do
The way these legs are moving
It's not pretty but it's soothing

Yesterday I was groovin' like a hula hoop
But it's okay to feel like this sometimes
Sticky, thick and slow
There's nowhere else I'd rather go.

The Universe

I feel like the energy in the universe
Ebbs and flows
And as hard as I try to predict
Or influence
When that will be
I am constantly surprised
When the tide chooses to rise.
Today was one of those days
For no particular reason
Things just worked
It wasn't perfect
Nothing miraculous happened
I didn't win the lottery
It was just a good
Old-fashioned
Easy going day

I wish I knew how to make that happen more often
I wish more people had days like that
But if I can't tap into the frequency
Where these things happen
The least I can do
Is remind myself that they do
And to know that it will always come back around
It's not an excuse for inaction
I know you have to make your own luck
I don't show up to a race without training
But I swear
There is something in the air
That causes the tide to rise higher
Randomly
And I hope I am always ready to witness
Without questioning
Or dissecting
Joy.

Do The Words Run

When you write
Do the words run
Do they skip to get
Ahead of you
Do they stop and wink
And tickle you
Keep up
It's time to go
The sun doesn't wait to rise
And the moon doesn't
Stop to say goodbye
Pause to collect your
Thoughts
But not for long
When you write
If you're lucky
The words will run ahead
Of you
And you'll spend the rest
Of your life
Chasing them.

The Laundry that Never Dries

The laundry that never dries
Haunts me
I dream about bibs hanging
From the ceiling fan
A jersey zipper tickling the
Radiator
Leg warmers stretched over
The last empty chair
They wish they were taller
The arm warmers are reaching
For something
The meaning of life?
I don't know
My mismatched socks are the real
Lost souls of the cycling world
Over the warmers,
Under the warmers?
It's a daily struggle.

SELF PRES ERVA TION

A Puff of Gatorade

A puff of Gatorade
Stops me in my tracks
How many times a day
Do I pour a scoop of drink mix
Into the bottle of water
Rushed, without blinking
On the go to the next thing
This is a split second of self-care
Self-preservation
The minimum recovery I might have
How have I never noticed the depth
Of this small cloud of dust
How it swirls
Seems to hover with hesitation
I don't have time for this
I can't see what I'm doing
I swipe it away
Irritated
But the simple monotony
Is beautiful
If you pay attention
If you notice the way
One action can linger
It can take your breath away.

How to Sit with Sitting Still

Take a deep breath
Close your eyes
Listen to the birds chirping
Breathe out
Notice that nothing around you
Is still
Notice how the gentle wind
Fluffs the tallest tree
Notice how
When you are still
You are no longer other
You are a part of the landscape
The blue bird sings
To you
Not despite you
The skies seem to brighten
If you're brave enough to
Sit still
To notice the motion around you
The flurry of natural occurrences
You'll notice the only thing
That's still
Is what's behind your eyes
Your sensitive, sensitive mind.

Breakfast Is a Ballet

Did you know I make the best
Egg sandwiches
It's about the order
And keeping everything warm
It's a delicate balance
I never said I was a professional chef
But I like eating
So
Sunny side up
How else do you greet the morning
Salt, pepper, oregano
Paprika
Whatever makes you feel spicy
Now
You need a soft cheese
Something that will melt quickly
No fuss

This is a sandwich not a ballet
Fresh tomatoes
Or an avocado
If you've courted it properly
At least three dates
Something that can double as protein
and salt
Prosciutto
How I love you
Slice it thinly
No slurping
Next
Toast the bread
After the eggs
It should have a hint of mayonnaise
To lubricate the plate
If reading a menu
Doesn't feel like reading poetry
Don't eat it.

Sensations

No one talks about how hard it is
To perform
Even when you've done the work
You centre your whole life around
One thing
One goal
And you eat right
You sleep right
You have a part time job
That lets you ride
Mid-morning

And you're telling me
It all comes down to
Sensations -
What kind of voodoo magic is that?

Tell me where you get them
Do you buy them online
A boutique fitness store
The back corner of
Your favourite bike shop

On the street before the
Saturday group ride
Do you collect them
In the forest
On a long solo off-road
Death march
Where you find yourself
But sensations elude you

Do you find them in your
Morning coffee
With beans ground by hand
In the perfect pancake
With bananas that were too ripe
To be ride food
That's its own special sensation
But not what I'm looking for

Do you have travelling
Sensations
Down your arms or in your toes
You wake up and you know
That's just how sensations go.

Gather yourself
and all of your
anxiety,
Whisper to it
softly,
this is an
adventure.

How to surprise yourself

First
Forget everything you think you know
Sprinkle hope and excitement
On your eyelids
And then close them
Next
Gather yourself and all of your anxiety
Whisper to it softly
This is an adventure
We are here to have fun
Then
Imagine a blank slate
Reframe your mind
You are not all of your failures
You are a masterpiece
You are shades of a sunset
No one has ever seen before
You are more than you have been before
You are everything you dream about
Late at night
You are everyone you haven't met yet
You just have to be patient
I promise it's worth the wait.

I Am Not an Indoor Cat

I used to hate taking out the compost
When I was a kid
It's smelly and sticky and our driveway was long
I was always active
But outside scheduled practices
God forbid I move a muscle.

But I am not an indoor cat
It's so strange now I spend more time outside
Than I ever have
But my tolerance for spending time inside
Is extremely low

I feel antsy
Stiff
Anxious
Claustrophobic
I feel stale.
I need sunlight
As I get older I feel like I'm
Approaching photosynthesis
I understand the plants
I am in tune with the compost
I look forward to filling it up so I have an excuse
To get outside
And look up at the sky

I am not an indoor cat.

HOTO
YNTH
ESIS

I Didn't Want to be a Writer

I thought I didn't want to be
A writer
I didn't want to fight with
My ideas
But I'd rather fight with
My ideas
Try to herd the cats
Insatiable
Curious
Clinging things
Than force myself to think
About others singing
While I sit here writing
Crafty
Passive aggressive
Little time to blink
Sinking pit of your stomach
Emails about things
That keep me up at night
Not with excitement
But with blame
Because I settled for things to
Stay the same.

A Small Dose of Poetry

Everyone likes a small dose
Of poetry
On special occasions
Weddings, birthdays,
Baby showers
Maybe on the weekend
I don't know why
No one wants to feel that much
That often
I'd rather sink into my feelings
And let the words
Lift the weight
From my mind
I don't need to emotionally
Prepare to standstill
And breathe
The fight or flight
Away
I welcome it.

Forget everything you think you know.

Grab It, Don't Let Go

What is inspiration really
Is it a song you can't
Get out of your head
Is it purposely holding your breath?
Is it trying to remember
The first splash of summer
Again and again
Until memory feels like habit
Is it the wish on a shooting star
Please,
Can I be the constellation
Praying
On a runaway train
You better catch before its gone
The spark won't wait to hit you again
If you have an inkling
A tingling
A sense that someone
Is giggling
Grab it, don't let go.

My Problem with Social Media

I'm realizing maybe my problem with social media
Isn't lack of creativity
But an urge to be unique
Authentic is a word that isn't cool to throw around anymore
It's overused
I know I don't have to do anything mind bending
For you to know I like riding my bike
I go a lot of cool places
I drink coffee sometimes
And I train my ass off
But for some reason I'm convinced I have to be perfect
I have to be new
I have to be attractive when I'm happy
Even if I'm sweaty and dirty and bruised
And probably exhausted
Because after you have the ride of your life
Let's be honest
We are all of those things
We are not photogenic
We are not about posing
About taking shots over and over
To get the right light
The glow that tells you
I work out at the same time everyday
And I'm always motivated.
I want you to think all of these things
But I want you to know they aren't true
I want you to know
I'm just the same as you.

Chronic Thinker

Over thinker
Under thinker
I like to tinker with my
Ideas
Entertain my
Paranoia
Sink my teeth into
A good story
About why I'm not
Good enough
But I never find
An ending I like
I run out of reasons
To give in
To being mediocre
Despite everything,
I still have hope
I can do
Something great.

Sunlight

Do you ever catch the sunlight
Winking on your eyelid
The belly of the leaves
Falling
Shining with an ease

Do you ever catch the songbird
Waking in the day
Introduce a golden ray,
It's time to get out of the shade-

Open the windows
Let the cat go wild
Let her little whiskers shiver
And look higher, higher

It's a good day to go outside.

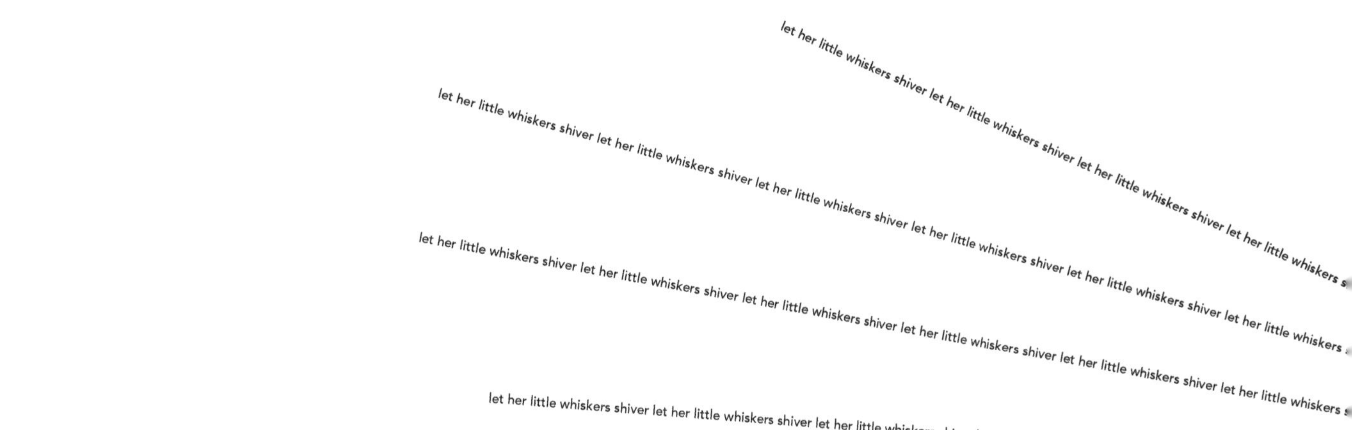

let her little whiskers shiver let her little whiskers shiver let her little whiskers shiver let her little whiskers
let her little whiskers shiver let her little whiskers shiver let her little whiskers shiver let her little whiskers shiver let her little whiskers shiver let her little whiskers shiver let her little whiskers
let her little whiskers shiver let her little whiskers shiver let her little whiskers shiver let her little whiskers shiver let her little whiskers shiver let her little whiskers shiver let her little whiskers
let her little whiskers shiver let her little whiskers shiver let her little whiskers shiver let her little whiskers shiver let her little whiskers shiver let her little whiskers shiver let her l
let her little whiskers shiver let her little whiskers shiver let her little whiskers shiver let her little whiskers shiver let her little whiskers shiver let her little whiskers
let her little whiskers shiver let her little whiskers shiver let her little whiskers shiver let her little whiskers shiver let her little whiskers shiver
let her little whiskers shiver let her little whiskers shiver let her little whiskers shiver let her litt

Joy will challenge you to the world's longest staring contest and blink first.

Joy is Lazy

No one has the guts to say it but
Joy is lazy
Joy is not easily impressed
Joy is easily amused but
Not a fan of quick fixes
Joy is in it for the long haul
Joy will challenge you to the world's
Longest staring contest
And blink first
Not good enough
Not cool
Not interested
Joy is the worst roommate
Joy has high expectations
And doesn't do the dishes
Joy is a mystery I'll spend my whole life
Trying to solve
When I look hard enough
I get lost
And joy finds me
In the strangest place.

Coffee Ride

I used to drink coffee just to fit in
Doesn't sound so bad
But the ultimate sign of maturity is declining things
That you'll regret later
It can be as simple as staying out late
Spending more money than you should
Spending too much time on your phone
Not making time for yourself
Not making time for yourself

I felt really left out of coffee rides because I didn't like coffee
And I felt like drinking coffee was a key personality trait
Cyclists are supposed to have
But it's not about that
It's about the sense of calm that comes with sitting down with your friends
Eating something yummy
Drinking something hot with your helmet on
And not taking life too seriously.

Winter Content

Winter content like sunshine
Bluebird skies
Crisp visibility
Snow that sits quietly
When you blow a kiss
Winter content like I'm so happy I can't feel my fingers
I'm so happy my cheeks
Are a permanent rose
It's the opposite of glowing.
I feel like my toes are on fire when I
Finally, gingerly,
Soak them in hot water
What else do you crave for hours that
Just ends up back firing?
You want winter content like
How long does it take for you to get dressed
How many pairs of pants do you wear
How many base layers
How many times
Do you
Take it all off to pee
Because you're nervous about
Freezing your teeth off?

I want winter content like
I was dressed perfectly
I'm glad I didn't ride inside
That I saw the forecast and thought –
Optimism will keep me warm
Hot apple cider
Hot chocolate
Whatever fills your belly with hope
Sometimes it feels like
A superpower
To be warm
When it's cold
You're defying nature
This generator runs on mental watts
And willpower
The beauty in professing this
Salt and slime
Is totally rideable
Imagine traction and it's there
Imagine a momentum the strongest headwind
Can't slow
You come back knowing
It made you stronger
Next time you can go even longer
That's the winter content I can give you.

Dream Big

But don't be afraid to talk back
To ask questions
To wonder if the dream still fits
If it feels heavy
If it needs a belt
If it chafes at the ankles
If sometimes you wish you could
Take it off
And try something new
Something more you
Gleeful
Dizzy with delight
Sweet as a secret you can't keep
Dream big enough
That an air balloon would burst
With excitement
A dream that keeps you wondering
What if
Not when
Not why
A dream you don't dare hide.

acklesnapc
snapcrackle
acklesnapc
snapcrackle
acklesnapcr
napcrackle
acklesnapcr
napcrackle
acklesnapcr

She's a Firecracker

Snap
Crackle
Paprika
Pretend you're
On the far side
Of a slingshot
Fling yourself
Eyes wide open
Into opportunity
Be brave enough
To risk falling short
We all saw the fireworks
And the splash you made afterwards.

Play to Your Strengths

Play to your strengths
But play to possibility too
Look it square in the eyes
And say I dare you
I dare you to test me
To be big and scary
And forgetful
To forget that I am
Not done growing
I am at home in bad weather
And fast-changing conditions
In the belief that I don't yet
Know my limits
I am a fistful of possibility.

Play to possibility too.

Small Wins

I'm a fan of small wins
Bite-sized adversity
Doing the thing
Even though I spilled my coffee
Before it was coffee
Even though I forgot to water the plants
Forgot to water myself
Forgot to turn on the toaster
Forgot to drink my tea when it was warm
I forgot to check the weather
I didn't know it could rain this hard
This long
Stubbing the ever-living shit
Out of my toe
Chomping so hard on my tongue
That I sink to my knees
Nutella and blood
An extracurricular chemistry class
I didn't sign up for
I want the little things
At the wrong time
To be the last fuck
My bucket could hold
And then doing the hard thing anyway
That's my small win for the day.

Life is Like a Winter Group Ride

You start off nervous and worried
You did everything you could think of to prepare
You padded your resume
Your ears and extremities
And still, you're a little shaky

Sometimes you forget to do your homework
Or let's be honest
Actively avoid it
And you show up with a false sense of bravado
Hoping that'll do the trick
It'll start off fast
In an attempt to shock your system
Scare you into giving up
What you don't know
Is more often than not
Just as your legs are burning
Your fingers hurt
And there's stuff you can't see
Slapping you in the face –
They'll slow down
Just enough to get a breather
But sometimes that's all you need
To keep up.

Just as your legs
Are burning
Your fingers hurt
And there's stuff
You can't see
Slapping you in
The face,
They'll slow down.

And I started to wonder if I really like cycling at all.

Resistance

I was riding my bike outside
For the first time in awhile
And I was supposed to be
Fresh as a daisy
Grinning ear to ear
I found myself staring at my front wheel
As it weaved in and out
Of the soft tire track
Already imprinted
In the not-frozen dirt
The cold wind scraped at my cheeks
And I started to wonder if I really like cycling
At all

What a time to have a crisis
10km out on a dead-end trail
I could bail soon,
In a few kilometres
Onto the salt-painted road
It would be colder
But at least the wind would be
Coming from behind
And if the pavement is soft
That's a bigger problem
Than positive thinking can solve.
And I have to say, once I used
My brain to chase something
Slightly less difficult
I realized my philosophical crisis
About my purpose in life
Was purely situational
If you're struggling
Find a way to give yourself
A little less resistance
And it will multiply.

Part Bike Robot

I like sunshine and scenery
Just as much as anyone else
I like New Road Day
And the way adventures unfurl
In the most unexpected ways
I like sitting at the café in my chamois
Much longer than I should
Sometimes I visualize fungi
Growing on my thighs.
And I close my eyes
As the sun dries the sweat on my rosy cheeks
My freckles greet the goosebumps on my
Shoulder
There's a thousand signs telling me
It's time to go
But still I sit and bask in silence
I'm so happy I could die.

I live vicariously
Through carefully planned and hand-picked
Watt bombs
Knowing my exact heart rate
When the perceived effort of pedalling
Through snow
Blows my threshold out of the water
I'm a simple woman
I get excited when TrainingPeaks is green

But is it the right kind of work
I have the thirst to complete
Does the pow check the boxes
Does it make me sweat
Does it cure the questioning
Of my constantly calculating mind
Do the numbers add up
To the exact TSS that will make me
Hate my bike
Just in time for a rest week
If I can ride the trainer
This hard
This long
With no trails in sight
Just the endless digital horizon
Imagine what I can do
With sunshine and scenery
And mountains and glee

I'll be laughing
That's the bike robot dream.

I like sitting at the café in my chamois
Much longer than I should
Sometimes I visualize fungi
Growing on my thighs.

BULL
BULL
BULL

Some Days I Feel Like I Just Learned to Walk

Some days I feel like
I just learned to walk
A weary fawn
Easily startled, off-balance
Forget cow-tipping
A sneeze could knock me down
But some days
I feel like a bull
I don't care what happens
Who's who -
Where?
I show up raging
Anyway
It would take a lot to phase me -
To take away the fire I have now.

The Grind

You need slow days
You need perfectly paced
Sloth-like
Are you really only going to do three things
Today
Days
Write some poetry
Go to the grocery store
Do some minor bike maintenance
And go for a spin
Probably do some work
Yeah, the stuff you've been avoiding all week
But today is so light
You don't even mind
'the grind'.

You need slow days

And you need days where you do
Even more nothing than that
That make you question what you're doing
And if you have any time to consider what you
Would like to be doing
That's the time to decide
Because it's not a grind if you like it.

What If I Can

Imagine doing something new
Something you thought you could never do
Something big and scary
Something you could fail
Fabulously
But what if you didn't
What if the idea makes you go wild
A fire in the corner of your eye
And instead of stomping it out
You gently blow belief
And feed it whole grains
A steady drip of commitment
And a sip of courage
Of anything can happen
Lady luck is fickle
So, bring pickles
In case you cramp
But damn,
I'd say you're ready
If you think
What if I can
Instead of
What if I can't?

What if I can
instead of
what if I can't?

About Mackenzie Myatt

I write about the idiosyncrasies of chasing excellence in sport and in life. For as long as I can remember, I have been writing poetry to process the world around me. I was a pretty shy, anxious kid and writing was the best way I knew express myself. In my teenage years, poetry became a lifeline for all of the things I couldn't say out loud. Now, it is the best way I know how to share all of the things that inspire me.

I have been active and competitive for as long as I can remember. I was a gymnast for 10 years before I decided to try to make it in cycling. My U23 years saw several invitations to National Team projects, World Cup projects, World Championships, Top-20 performances in Europe and National Championship podiums in Canada and the US. Collegiate racing gave me the perfect environment to practice racing to win, an education and many cherished memories. I currently race whatever events excite me, no matter the discipline.

I have a BFA in Writing from the Savannah College of Art and Design – Atlanta and split my time between my hometown, Musquodoboit Harbour, Nova Scotia and Georgia.

Acknowledgments

I want to thank my parents for always believing in me and supporting my big dreams. I certainly would not have made it this far without you.

I want to thank my husband, Artúr for believing in me always. Especially when I wanted to give up, he helped me fall in love with the sport again. He suggested that I put my two favourite things together and see what happens. Thank you for your patience, your unconditional love, and your passion for life.

Thank you to Molly Hurford and Strong Girl Publishing for giving my work a home and an avenue to inspire girls everywhere. Thank you for believing in me as a writer AND an athlete. Thank you for being a friend, a mentor and just generally being a badass. Your podcast The Business of Fitness inspired me to dream differently.

Thank you to Alison Testroete of Athlete to Enterprise for encouraging me to dream big. Just applying for the program motivated me to start sharing my work. Thank you to Global Relay - Bridge The Gap Fund & supporters for funding four scholarships; I would not have been able to participate otherwise. Thank you to Leah Kirchman for facilitating that opportunity and for showing up in many different ways and places for me this year. Your enthusiasm is contagious.

Thank you to Geweldige Meiden op de Fiets Youth Cycling Team in Dartmouth, NS for allowing me to share my experience and my love for the sport with you. As long as you're having fun, you're on the right track!

Thank you to Andrew Feenstra and Cyclesmith Halifax for supporting me throughout my journey. I would not be where I am today without the Cyclesmith Short Track Series and the Cyclesmith Junior Racing Team.

Thank you to Sharleen Hoar and Dan Proulx for believing in me and thank you to Catharine Pendrel for inspiring me from the very beginning.

Thank you to my family, friends, competitors and everyone else who has supported me along the way!